ZATHORI'S SPELL

Jadine Tyne

www.JadineTyne.com

First Edition: October 2017.

You can buy copies of this publication at **Amazon** or by contacting the author through her website: **www.JadineTyne.com**

Cover design by María José Martín García: www.instagram.com/majoworks7

To Antonio
And Leo.

Contents

Foreword
Written by Roger Orr

Samantha and Damasco – just another young couple looking forward to the birth of their first child, but a couple versed in telepathic and magical powers. In Jadine Tyne's screenplay, the dividing line between reality and fantasy is breached repeatedly, but far from being fantasia characters, Tyne's characters are real people with real jobs and real day to day issues – the only difference is they can influence both the present and the future with their magical powers.

When Samantha inadvertently stumbles telepathically across a murder plot reminding the reader of events in Coppola's "The Conversation", the screenplay kicks into high gear on magical power – no hybrid motors required for Tyne to maintain the suspense. A morality tale unfolds, in which the puzzle which life is addressed through experiences, perceptions and above all, decision making. Will Tyne's characters do the right thing or succumb to the temptation of the powers they hold?

Read on. Many new writers are seductive and
provocative. Few show the tenderness of Tyne
when writing about Samantha, Damasco and
others. Be they treasured friends from her
life or from the vaults of her rich
imagination, their spectral quality will
remain with you long after you put down this
screenplay.

Roger Orr

Zathori's Spell

Pilot Episode:

Magic's Back

COLD OPEN

EXT. PARK - DAY

YOUNG SAMANTHA is 8 years old and is looking
at some trees. She is wearing a PENDANT which
consists in a jade oval. Her hand touches the
pendant and it starts to shine.

> YOUNGER BLANCA (OS)
> *Sam?*

SAMANTHA blinks and takes her hand off the
PENDANT. SAMANTHA turns around and sees
YOUNGER BLANCA, who looks 38 years old.

> YOUNGER BLANCA
> Let's go home. Your grandpa
> is waiting for us.

SAMANTHA runs towards BLANCA.

INT. BLANCA'S LIVING ROOM - NIGHT

The living room is spacious: there are two
settees and a couch with a glass table before
the settees. YOUNGER BLANCA is on one couch
and YOUNG SAMANTHA is sat down on the other
couch with YOUNGER LEOPOLDO, who is 65 years
old. YOUNG SAMANTHA yawns.

> YOUNGER BLANCA
> You should go to bed.

SAMANTHA yawns again.

                    YOUNG SAMANTHA
          I'm not tired.

                    YOUNGER LEOPOLDO
          Come on, señorita, do as
          your mother says. I'll read
          you a story.

YOUNG SAMANTHA smiles, stands up and kisses
good-night to YOUNGER BLANCA.

YOUNG SAMANTHA exits the living room followed
by YOUNGER LEOPOLDO.

INT. SAMANTHA'S BEDROOM - NIGHT

YOUNGER SAMANTHA closes her eyes. She is on
the bed.

YOUNGER LEOPOLDO closes the book and leaves it
on a bedside table. YOUNGER LEOPOLDO leans
forward YOUNG SAMANTHA and kisses her
forehead.

EXT. PARK - NIGHT

YOUNGER LEOPOLDO is looking at the trees YOUNG
SAMANTHA was looking at previously. YOUNGER
LEOPOLDO is carrying a TORCH in his hand and
pointing at those trees.

NERIUS appears from the trees. He is 35 years
old. He has dark hair and dark eyes. He is
dressed in black and he looks fit. NERIUS
looks at YOUNGER LEOPOLDO and smiles.

                    NERIUS
          Oh, Leopoldo, nice to see
          you again.

                    YOUNGER LEOPOLDO
          What do you need, Nerius?

                    NERIUS
          Come to Zathori. We need
          you.

                    YOUNGER LEOPOLDO
          I can't go yet. You must
          wait.

                    NERIUS
          But.. Oh... Who's that?

YOUNGER LEOPOLDO turns his head and sees YOUNG
SAMANTHA dressed in her pyjamas, with a teddy
bear under her arm. YOUNGER LEOPOLDO looks at
NERIUS.

                    YOUNGER LEOPOLDO
          Go back now. We'll talk
          soon.

NERIUS heads into the trees and disappears.
YOUNGER LEOPOLDO turns around and goes towards
YOUNG SAMANTHA.

                    YOUNGER LEOPOLDO (CONT'D)
          Sam...

YOUNGER LEOPOLDO takes YOUNG SAMANTHA in his
arms.

                    YOUNG SAMANTHA
          Abuelo...

                END OF COLD OPEN

ACT 1

EXT. MADRID - MORNING

The sun is rising. A pale reddish glow glints off the building surrounded by the squares and parks of Madrid city: El Retiro park, Colón square, La Cibeles square, Picasso Tower, General Perón Park and the British Council building.

There is a building, a window.

INT. BEDROOM - NIGHT

On the right side of the window there are some shelves with books and boxes. There is also a LAPTOP on a table, a notebook with a pen next to the laptop, and a chair. There is a PICTURE of DAMASCO (19) and SAMANTHA (15) on the wall above the table.

On the left side of the window the bed is placed. DAMASCO (34) is on top of SAMANTHA (30), they are covered with the bed sheet. DAMASCO rolls back to his side of the bed. He is smiling.

> DAMASCO
> Good morning to you too.

SAMANTHA is smiling.

INT. DAMASCO'S STUDY - NIGHT

There is a table with a screen and a keyboard
on it. There is also a LAPTOP. There is a CPU
under the table and an office chair in front
of the table. On the left side of the table
there are some shelves with books of different
topics: comics, information technology,
countries... There are also some boxes.

INT. KITCHEN - NIGHT

The kitchen is large. On one side there is a
counter top with a small dishwasher below it,
a kitchen sink and a cupboard below it,
another countertop, a refrigerator, an
electric cooker with an oven below, and
another countertop with drawers below. On the
other side there is a small table and two
chairs.

DAMASCO enters the kitchen. He is dressed in a
pair of jeans, a white t-shirt and slippers.

INT. BEDROOM - NIGHT

SAMANTHA is finishing making the bed. She is
dressed in a pair of dark trousers and a
shirt. When she finishes making the bed she
sits down and puts some comfortable shoes on.

                    DAMASCO (OS)
          Sam???? Tea is ready.

SAMANTHA smiles.

INT. KITCHEN - NIGHT

SAMANTHA is sat down on one of the chairs.
DAMASCO gives a cup of tea to SAMANTHA. She
puts it on the table. SAMANTHA stands up and
kisses DAMASCO. He kisses her back and
caresses her womb.

INT. BEDROOM - NIGHT

SAMANTHA takes her BAG. She takes a book and
the keys that are on the table and put it all
inside her BAG.

INT. DAMASCO'S STUDY - NIGHT

DAMASCO is typing some HTML code on his
computer. SAMANTHA appears.

                    SAMANTHA
          Darling, I'm off to work.

DAMASCO stops typing, turns around, stands up
and approaches SAMANTHA. They embrace and
kiss.

                    DAMASCO
          Don't work hard.

                    SAMANTHA
          Okay. And you take a break
          from time to time.

                    DAMASCO
          Okay.

They smile and kiss again.

EXT. ALCALÁ STREET - DAY

SAMANTHA exits from the underground stop
called "Suanzes", walks straight and enters a
cafeteria called "Nostrum".

INT. NOSTRUM CAFETERIA - DAY

The cafeteria is a wide space and there is
plenty of light. There are food and drinks
refrigerated on several shelves. There are
customers at tables having breakfast.

PACO (48) and TAYRI (46) have dark hair and
they both dress in black. PACO is pouring milk
into a cup while TAYRI is placing a muffin on
a tray. A CUSTOMER is waiting for them to
finish serving the breakfast.

SAMANTHA enters the cafeteria, goes to a
refrigerated shelf, picks a bottle of still
water and goes to the till. PACO and TAYRI see
SAMANTHA and they both smile.

                    PACO
          Buenos días, ¿cómo estás tú?

                    TAYRI
          Buenos días belleza.

                    SAMANTHA
          Buenos días pareja.

SAMANTHA pays in cash and TAYRI takes the
money.

                    PACO
          Did you get inspired?

SAMANTHA
I did indeed. I found time
to finish reading the book.

TAYRI
How did you do it if you
fall asleep so often?

SAMANTHA
Well, I don't get that tired
now, lucky me. I can do more
things.

PACO
Good for you!

TAYRI
Just one bit of advice: Have
a rest whenever you need it.

PACO
And if you need it at work,
just leave your desk and
hide somewhere. You can ask
Nora to play hide and seek
with you.

SAMANTHA
(laughs) Yes, I'll rest when
I need it. (laughs) Well,
now I must leave to apply my
inspiration to the book
review. Hasta luego pareja.

PACO
Nos vemos luego.

                         TAYRI
                Hasta luego preciosa.

SAMANTHA goes to the exit.

EXT. ALCALÁ STREET - DAY

SAMANTHA exits the cafeteria and turns to the
right.

EXT. MIGUEL YUSTE STREET - DAY

SAMANTHA walks down the street.

SAMANTHA enters the "Booking Books" building.

INT. OFFICE - DAY

There are office chairs and a lot of tables
with screens, keyboards, mouses, laptops and
telephones on them. There are plants, bottles,
cups and books on some of the tables. There
are some people working with their computers,
other people are talking and having coffee.

SAMANTHA sits at her desk and NORA appears.
NORA is 30 years old, has blonde hair and is
slim.

                         NORA
                Good moooorniiinnggg.

                       SAMANTHA
                Morning!

SAMANTHA turns the computer on while NORA sits
on the table.

                    NORA
          How was your weekend? Did
          you do something special?

                  SAMANTHA
          I slept a lot and I also
          finished reading the book.

                    NORA
          Good! Which one are you
          reviewing today? Don't tell
          me. Wait, wait,... "What To
          Expect When You're
          Expecting".

                  SAMANTHA
          (laughs) Nooooo. It's "Get
          Inspired" by Pancho Campo.
          It is about how to reduce
          stress and talks about four
          kind of energies: physical,
          mental, emotional and
          spiritual. The most
          important thing is to keep
          them in balance. So we must
          watch out when one of them
          is running low.

                    NORA
          Interesting... Imagine if
          you could make an energy
          ball and throw it to
          yourself or anybody else in
          order to charge the energy
          needed. It would be cool.

SAMANTHA
Hummmm... I don't think
so... Anyway, what book are
you going to write about?
Wait, wait, don't tell me. I
guess you had a thrilling
weekend so the book must be
a Jules Verne. It could
be... "Twenty Thousand
Leagues Under the Sea".
Or... "Journey to the Centre
of the Earth".

NORA
(laughs) Noooooooooo. I
didn't have a thrilling
weekend. (laughs). It's "Why
Not?" by Aileen Diolch. It's
a short story about a woman
who realises her dream of
running her own business.
She takes a few days off to
go to her sister's wedding.
She meets an ex-boyfriend,
the love of her life, and
they realise they are still
in love. Tataaaahhh.

SAMANTHA
Another love story. You
really like romantic books.

NORA
I don't get tired of these
books...

SAMANTHA
One day you'll find your
perfect match.

                    NORA
          Maybe... Today I have a
          date... We'll see...

NORA goes to her desk while SAMANTHA is
looking at her.

SAMANTHA is typing. She closes her eyes.

FLASHBACK

EXT. RETIRO PARK - DAY

There is a small waterfall. The sky is gray
and it begins to rain. The waterfall gets
closer and there are raindrops falling into
the small POND.

YOUNG SAMANTHA is wearing wellington boots and
an anorak. She throws her ball into the lake
and stares at it. She turns around.

YOUNGER BLANCA is also wearing wellington
boots and an anorak. She shakes her head.

                 YOUNGER BLANCA
          Sam, why did you throw the
          ball into the pond? It is
          raining and you will either
          get wet or come back home
          without the ball.

                 YOUNG SAMANTHA
          Mum, I have my wellies on.

                 YOUNGER BLANCA

You don't know how deep that
pond is.

                YOUNG SAMANTHA
I'm wet anyway.

                YOUNGER BLANCA
I don't approve.

                YOUNG SAMANTHA
Okay, I'll look for a stick.

                YOUNGER BLANCA
And if you don't find one?

                YOUNG SAMANTHA
I'll leave the ball in the
pond.

                YOUNGER BLANCA
Are you sure?

                YOUNG SAMANTHA
Mum, it's just a ball.

END OF FLASHBACK

INT. OFFICE - DAY

SAMANTHA opens her eyes, takes her bottle and
drinks water. NORA appears.

                NORA
Did you fall asleep again?

                SAMANTHA
I can't avoid it.

                    NORA
          It's because you write about
          boring books and you get
          bored.

SAMANTHA stares at NORA.

                    NORA (CONT'D)
          (laughs) It's a joke! I find
          quite interesting your last
          read. I am interested.
          Really.

                    SAMANTHA
          Nora, I have just had
          another flashback...

                    NORA
          Okay. You need a break. Come
          with me.

EXT. NOSTRUM CAFETERIA - DAY

SAMANTHA and NORA are seated in the terrace of
the cafeteria. SAMANTHA is drinking orange
juice and NORA is sipping her coffee. TAYRI
comes out with two muffins.

                    TAYRI
          Two sweet muffins for my two
          sweet girls.

TAYRI serves the muffins while SAMANTHA and
NORA smile at her.

                    NORA
          Gracias.

                    SAMANTHA
          Gracias.

TAYRI goes inside.

                    NORA
          You don't need to worry.
          Perhaps you miss your mum
          more now that you are
          pregnant.

                    SAMANTHA
          You are so sweet. I think
          I'm going to cry.

                    NORA
          See? Hormones...

                    SAMANTHA
          Yes... Perhaps you are
          right...

                    NORA
          Of course!!

SAMANTHA and NORA smile and hug.

INT. NOSTRUM CAFETERIA - DAY

SAMANTHA and NORA come inside and go to the
till. NORA pays in cash.

                    TAYRI
          Nos vemos luego, bellezas.

                    SAMANTHA
          Yes!!

ANDREW (28) enters the cafeteria. He is an
attractive young man.

                    PACO
          Ohhh. You're here early.

SAMANTHA and NORA turn around and see ANDREW.

                    NORA
          Hello there...

                    PACO
          This is our new employee.
          His name is Andrew. Andrew:
          Meet Samantha and Nora.

ANDREW is staring at NORA.

                    ANDREW
          Nice to meet you.

NORA is smiling widely. SAMANTHA takes her by
her arm.

                    SAMANTHA
          We must go now. See you at
          lunch.

SAMANTHA hurries to the exit while NORA can't
take her eyes off ANDREW.

INT. OFFICE - DAY

NORA is leaving Samantha's desk.

                    SAMANTHA

Try to pretend you are not
that interested in him.

                  NORA
My hormones are partying...

                SAMANTHA
You, single woman, remember
that tonight you have a
date.

                  NORA
You are being supportive.
Thanks!

NORA winks at SAMANTHA and goes to her desk.
SAMANTHA is smiling.

SAMANTHA is at her desk. She leaves the bottle
of still water on the table and starts typing.

              LEOPOLDO (OS)
     Sam...

Everything goes black.

END OF ACT 1

ACT 2

INT. HOSPITAL ROOM - NIGHT

SAMANTHA is at the hospital, sleeping on a
bed. NORA is next to her, sat down on a couch,
fiddling with her smartphone. The room is very
spacious: there is a window, a door, a
wardrobe, a table with two chairs and a small
table beside the couch.

DAMASCO enters the room.

> DAMASCO
> (whispering)
> *Nora...*

NORA looks at him and smiles. She leaves the
smartphone on the table next to her, stands up
and goes towards DAMASCO. NORA and DAMASCO
embrace.

> NORA
> Sam and the baby are fine.

DAMASCO smiles and embraces NORA again.

> DAMASCO
> That's good news.

SAMANTHA opens her eyes.

> SAMANTHA
> (whispering)
> *Damasco...*

DAMASCO approaches SAMANTHA, takes her hand in both of his and kisses her forehead.

The DOCTOR (60) enters the bedroom. He is wearing a white coat with some pens on his left breast pocket. He is also wearing a stethoscope around his neck. The DOCTOR approaches SAMANTHA.

                    DOCTOR
          How are you feeling?

                    SAMANTHA
          Good.

The DOCTOR examines SAMANTHA with his stethoscope.

                    DOCTOR
          Breathe normally... Hold
          on... Breathe again... Good.

The DOCTOR puts the stethoscope back on his neck.

                    DOCTOR (CONT'D)
          Everything is fine. You can
          go home now. By the way,
          would you like to know if
          the baby is a boy or a girl?

SAMANTHA, DAMASCO and NORA open their eyes wide and the three of them smile.

                    SAMANTHA
          Yes, please.

                    DAMASCO
          Yes.

NORA nods. The DOCTOR smiles.

                    DOCTOR
          It's a girl.

DAMASCO kisses SAMANTHA on the lips. NORA
kisses DAMASCO on the cheek and then kisses
SAMANTHA and gives her a hug.

                    DOCTOR (CONT'D)
          As I said before, you can go
          home but *(looking at
          SAMANTHA)* you need to rest
          and don't get stressed.

NORA looks at the DOCTOR.

                    NORA
          She already knows how to
          reduce stress.

NORA looks at SAMANTHA and smiles.

                    NORA (CONT'D)
          You just need to know which
          energy needs to be charged.

NORA winks at SAMANTHA.

EXT. HOSPITAL - DAY

SAMANTHA, DAMASCO and NORA are at the main
entrance of the hospital.

                    SAMANTHA
          Where did you park the car?

                    DAMASCO
          Just right behind Nora's.

SAMANTHA, DAMASCO and NORA walk along the
street until they reach a PINK CAR.

                    DAMASCO (CONT'D)
          You'll never lose your car.

                    NORA
          Noooo. I chose pink because
          it is an unusual colour for
          a car so I could find it
          easily.

                    DAMASCO
          You don't like pink a lot,
          do you?

                    NORA
          Not that much. But I don't
          like driving a lot either.
          I'd rather have someone to
          drive for me but, as long as
          I need a car, I want it to
          be easy to spot if I don't
          remember where I parked it.
          Pink is a very useful color,
          much more than your white
          car.

The WHITE CAR behind the PINK one is a TOYOTA
PRIUS.

                    DAMASCO
          Well, I prefer a discreet
          colour instead.

INT. BEDROOM - NIGHT

SAMANTHA is sitting on the bed sipping her cup
of tea. DAMASCO is next to her sipping his tea
from a mug. SAMANTHA leaves her cup on the
bedside table and lies down. DAMASCO stands
up, leaves his mug on the same table, kisses
SAMANTHA'S forehead, takes his mug and smiles
to SAMANTHA.

> DAMASCO
> Have a nice siesta,
> sweetheart.

> SAMANTHA
> Thank you, darling. I really
> need a nap.

DAMASCO kisses her lips and exits the room.
SAMANTHA closes her eyes.

FLASHBACK

EXT. RETIRO PARK - DAY

We see the pond with the small waterfall. It
is raining. Samantha's BALL is floating on the
pond.

> YOUNG SAMANTHA (OS)
> *Mum, it's just a ball.*

YOUNG NADOC, who is 10 years old, appears from
some trees. He is also wearing an anorak and
wellington boots. He has a butterfly net in
one of his hands.

                    YOUNG NADOC
          Hi.

YOUNGER BLANCA and YOUNG SAMANTHA look at
YOUNG NADOC, who is smiling.

                    YOUNG NADOC
          I can get your ball back
          with my butterfly net if you
          want.

NADOC rescues the ball from the pond and gives
it to SAMANTHA, who is smiling at him.

                    YOUNG SAMANTHA
          Thanks.

                    YOUNGER BLANCA
          Thank you very much.

END OF FLASHBACK

INT. BEDROOM - NIGHT

SAMANTHA is sat down on the bed and DAMASCO is
next to her.

                    SAMANTHA
          That's what Nora said about
          the previous flashback. But
          this time Nadoc was there.

                    DAMASCO
          Well,... Nadoc helped you a
          lot and you haven't heard
          anything about him since...

                    SAMANTHA
          I know, I know.

                    DAMASCO
          Maybe you miss him too.

                    SAMANTHA
          Or I miss my grandfather.

                    DAMASCO
          Yes, Nadoc helped you to
          find him and rescue me.
          Somehow he used to be the
          link between you and
          Leopoldo.

SAMANTHA smiles at DAMASCO.

                    SAMANTHA
          Link... What a metaphor...

DAMASCO smiles back at SAMANTHA.

                    DAMASCO
          And the target is blank
          because it opens a new
          world.

                    SAMANTHA
          And the title is "I help you
          out".

SAMANTHA looks at her hands.

                    SAMANTHA (CONT'D)
          Anyway, that was a long time
          ago. I enjoy my ordinary
          life with you.

SAMANTHA caresses her womb and smiles at
DAMASCO.

                    SAMANTHA (CONT'D)
          And our baby.

                    DAMASCO
          We will have to think of a
          name for her.

SAMANTHA and DAMASCO smile and kiss.

INT. KITCHEN - NIGHT

The lights are on. SAMANTHA and DAMASCO are
having supper.

INT. BEDROOM - NIGHT

SAMANTHA and DAMASCO are on the bed sleeping,
holding hands.

INT. UNDERGROUND - NIGHT

SAMANTHA is seated reading the book "Why Not?"
by Aileen Diolch.

INT. BOSS OFFICE - NIGHT

SAMANTHA is sitting on a chair. She is in a
big room that has a big window, a big desk
with a big chair.

The BOSS (50) enters the room. SAMANTHA turns her head to look at him and begins to stand up, the BOSS puts his hand on her shoulder. SAMANTHA sits down.

The BOSS sits down on his chair before SAMANTHA.

                    BOSS
          How do you feel? I heard you
          fainted while I was away.

                    SAMANTHA
          I feel better now. The
          doctor told me to have some
          days of rest and not get
          stressed.

                    BOSS
          Well, in that case you must
          do what the doctor told you.
          So... what are you doing
          here?

                    SAMANTHA
          I think I'm going to get
          bored at home so I thought I
          could do some work.

                    BOSS
          Oh, I see. Okay. What about
          reading a book? You know
          where the books to be read
          and reviewed are piled up.

                    SAMANTHA
          But I have some deadlines. I
          must write about the new
          author of Booking Books. The

magazines are waiting for
them.

                BOSS
I think one of your
colleagues can do it. You
need to rest, so, please,
just read one of the books
from the pile. Next week you
will have time to write
articles for the media and
go to presentations.

                SAMANTHA
Ooookaaaay. I'll pick two
books so I keep busy in my
relaxation time.

The BOSS looks at SAMANTHA and smiles. He
stands up. SAMANTHA stands up.

                BOSS
Good girl. See you next
week.

INT. OFFICE - DAY

SAMANTHA and NORA are talking. They are at
SAMANTHA's desk.

                SAMANTHA
So... it didn't go that
well.

                NORA
No, but it's okay. As you
told me, one day I'll find
my perfect match.

SAMANTHA takes two BOOKS that are on her table
and puts them in her bag.

                    NORA (CONT'D)
          Which books are you taking
          home?

                    SAMANTHA
          "Without Blood" by
          Alessandro Baricco and "The
          Yellow Bag" by Lygia Bojunga
          Nunes.

                    NORA
          The second one is for
          children...

                    SAMANTHA
          The main character is a
          girl.

                    NORA
          Perhaps you will like it for
          the baby... When she grows
          up and learns to read...

                    SAMANTHA
          (laughs) Of course. Anyway,
          I'm leaving now. I'm going
          home.

                    NORA
          Enjoy these days!

                    SAMANTHA
          I will...

NORA goes to her desk while SAMANTHA leaves
hers.

EXT. BOOKING BOOKS - DAY

SAMANTHA exits the building and walks up the
street.

INT. UNDERGROUND - NIGHT

SAMANTHA is sat down on a bench reading "Why
Not?" by Aileen Diolch.

The TRAIN arrives at the station. SAMANTHA
lifts her head, closes her BOOK, stands up and
steps towards the TRAIN.

The TRAIN stops and SAMANTHA opens the door
and enters.

INT. TRAIN - NIGHT

There are just MAN 1 and MAN 2 seated together
and the rest of the seats are empty. SAMANTHA
sits down close to the two men, opens her book
and reads.

> MAN 1 (OS)
> *It should be an easy task.*

> MAN 2 (OS)
> *Well, it's fuckin' well
> paid.*

SAMANTHA closes her book and stares at the
window in front of her.

                    MAN 1 (OS)
          *Yeah. They wan' us to act
          quickly.*

                    MAN 2 (OS)
          The sooner the better.

                    MAN 1 (OS)
          *Ya right. Easy job, easy
          money.*

SAMANTHA blinks her eyes.

                    MAN 2 (OS)
          Do ya have a pic of her?

                    MAN 1 (OS)
          Nope, they'll send it later.

SAMANTHA looks at the two men.

                    MAN 2
                (not moving his lips)
          But for now we can entertain
          some young ladies. I need to
          get laid.

                    MAN 1
                (not moving his lips)
          I want one with red hair.

SAMANTHA turns her head and opens her eyes
widely.

                    MAN 2 (OS)
          I want two at the same time.

Everything goes black.

END OF ACT 2

ACT 3

INT. DAMASCO'S STUDY - NIGHT

SAMANTHA is sitting on Damasco's office chair, DAMASCO is on a chair in front of SAMANTHA. SAMANTHA is crying.

>   DAMASCO
> Calm down, Sam. We'll get an
> answer.

DAMASCO hugs SAMANTHA. We hear the doorbell RINGING.

SAMANTHA and DAMASCO stand up and leave the study.

INT. LIVING ROOM - NIGHT

The living room has a window. There is a settee, a couch, a table between them, some shelves with a TV and a DVD player on one of them. There is also a door and a corridor.

DAMASCO and SAMANTHA enter the living room from the corridor.

INT.HALL - NIGHT

DAMASCO opens the door.

NADOC (32) is outside. He has a smiling face.

                         NADOC
          Hi.

INT. LIVING ROOM - NIGHT

SAMANTHA and DAMASCO are sitting on the settee
and NADOC is on the couch. On the table, there
are three mugs with plates below them.

EXT. NOSTRUM CAFETERIA - DAY

NORA exits the cafeteria. ANDREW follows NORA
with a plastic bag full of food.

NORA and ANDREW arrive at the PINK CAR. NORA
goes to the driver's door, inserts the key,
unlocks the car, goes to the boot and opens
it. ANDREW puts the plastic bag inside. NORA
closes the boot. NORA turns and sees ANDREW
staring at her.

                      ANDREW
          Maybe it's too soon but I'd
          like to see ya outside the
          cafe one day. We could go to
          the park, for example.

NORA opens her eyes widely.

                      ANDREW (CONT'D)
          Just... a walk. To get to
          know each other.

                      NORA
          You don't waste time, do
          you?

                    ANDREW
          No when it's somethin'
          important...

                    NORA
          Well... Now I must look
          after Sam...

                    ANDREW
          Maybe next week?

                    NORA
          Maybe.

NORA smiles and gets in her car. NORA starts
the engine and waves goodbye to ANDREW. NORA
leaves.

A BLACK CAR is parked, its engine starts and
it goes in the same direction as Nora's car.
When the BLACK CAR passes ANDREW, MAN 1 puts
two fingers to his eyebrow and then puts them
down. ANDREW nods.

EXT. STREET - DAY

NORA parks her PINK CAR. NORA exits the car.
NORA goes to the back of her car, opens the
boot, takes out the plastic bag, closes the
boot, goes to the driver's door, inserts a key
and locks the door.

The BLACK CAR is parked behind the pink one.
MAN 1 and MAN 2 watch NORA entering a
building.

INT. LIFT - NIGHT

NORA enters the lift.

INT. CORRIDOR - NIGHT

NORA is in front of a door.

INT. LIVING ROOM - NIGHT

SAMANTHA, DAMASCO and NADOC are talking. The
doorbell RINGS.

                    DAMASCO
          I'll go.

DAMASCO leaves the living room.

                    NADOC
          Is it a boy or a girl?

                    SAMANTHA
          How do you know...? Never
          mind. It's a girl.

DAMASCO enters the room followed by NORA. NORA
looks at NADOC. NADOC looks at NORA.

                    NORA
          Nadoc?

NADOC stands up while DAMASCO sits down next
to SAMANTHA. NADOC goes towards NORA.

                    NADOC
          Hi, Nora.

NADOC and NORA embrace.

                    SAMANTHA
          Dam, let's prepare some
          supper.

SAMANTHA and DAMASCO stand up.

NADOC and NORA are still embracing while
SAMANTHA and DAMASCO leave the living room.

INT. KITCHEN - NIGHT

SAMANTHA has a bowl of crisps in her hands and
NORA has a water pitcher.

                    SAMANTHA
          And I'm really going to
          rest.

                    NORA
          Just enjoy your relaxing
          cup...

                    SAMANTHA
          ... of café con leche...

                    NORA
          ... in Plaza Mayor.

SAMANTHA and NORA laugh.

SAMANTHA and NORA leave the kitchen.

INT. BLACK CAR - NIGHT

MAN 1 and MAN 2 are inside the car. MAN 2 is

sleeping. MAN 1 is looking at the building.

INT. LIVING ROOM - NIGHT

SAMANTHA, DAMASCO, NORA and NADOC are in the
living room, which has the lights on. DAMASCO
is sitting on the couch, SAMANTHA is on the
settee next to him, with NORA and NADOC on the
other side.

> SAMANTHA
> Perhaps I dreamt it all.
> Even if it was real, I don't
> want to have anything to do
> with magic.

> DAMASCO
> I understand.

> NADOC
> But it is something you
> can't avoid.

> NORA
> It's part of who you are.

> SAMANTHA
> *(looking at NORA and NADOC)*
> You two always liked magic.

> DAMASCO
> But they are right.

> SAMANTHA
> Yes...

> DAMASCO
> You just need to rest.

INT. BEDROOM - NIGHT

SAMANTHA and NORA are in the bedroom. SAMANTHA
is on the bed reading "Without Blood" by
Alessandro Baricco while NORA is sat down on
the couch reading "The Yellow Bag" by Lygia
Bojunga Nunes.

INT. BLACK CAR - NIGHT

A text message BEEPS. MAN 1 takes out his
smartphone and opens the message.

There is a picture of Samantha with her name
as a caption.

Samantha Freire, 30 years old.

MAN 1 turns off his smartphone. MAN 2 is still
sleeping.

                    MAN 1
          Wake up. It's time.

INT. LIVING ROOM - NIGHT

DAMASCO and NADOC are talking. DAMASCO is sat
down on the settee and NADOC on the couch.

                    DAMASCO
          ... and that's my job. So,
          what do you do for a living?

                    NADOC
          I am a personal trainer.

                    DAMASCO
          (laughs) You've become a
          personal trainer... Do you
          tell people how to get fit
          and that stuff?

                     NADOC
          Not just that. I also help
          people to manage their
          powers and also how to
          summon them.

                    DAMASCO
          Oh...

NORA enters the living room.

                     NORA
          Hi guys. The princess is
          sleeping.

NORA sits down next to DAMASCO.

                 NORA (CONT'D)
          So, did I miss something?

                    DAMASCO
          Nadoc has become a personal
          trainer.

                     NORA
          Good for you!!

The doorbell RINGS. NORA stands up and leaves
the room.

INT. HALL - NIGHT

NORA opens the door. MAN 1 is in front of
NORA. MAN 1 carries some books.

> MAN 1
> I've got these books for
> Miss Samantha Freire, ma'am.

> NORA
> She's busy at the moment but
> you can give them to me and
> she will have a look at them
> later.

> MAN 1
> Can't do it, ma'am. The
> publishin' company told me
> to deliver in person, a one-
> to-one relationship. Will
> come back tomorrow.

MAN 1 leaves and NORA closes the door.

INT. LIVING ROOM - NIGHT

NORA enters the living room and sits down on
the couch.

MAN 2 appears from the corridor. He has a GUN
on his hand and he is aiming at DAMASCO, NORA
and NADOC, who turn around to look at him. MAN
2 blinks his eyes and disappears. DAMASCO,
NORA and NADOC look at each other. DAMASCO and
NADOC stand up quickly.

> NADOC
> Nora...

                              NORA
                    What was that??

                             NADOC
                    Hide when they appear.

                             NORA
                    How do you know...?

                            DAMASCO
                    Do as he says, please!

MAN 1 and MAN 2 appear in front of DAMASCO,
NORA and NADOC, GUNS in their hands. NORA
stands up quickly.

                             NADOC
                    Hurry up!!

DAMASCO and NADOC cover NORA while she hides
behind the settee.

                        NADOC (CONT'D)
                    You, blinkers...

INT. BEDROOM - NIGHT

SAMANTHA is sleeping.

EXT. PARK - DAY

SAMANTHA is seated on a bench looking at the
pond. The sky is cloudy.

LEOPOLDO (85) appears from some bushes.
SAMANTHA looks at LEOPOLDO and smiles.
LEOPOLDO, smiles, goes towards SAMANTHA and
sits down next to her. LEOPOLDO and SAMANTHA
hug.

> SAMANTHA
> Abuelo... what are you doing
> here? This is not a
> flashback.

> LEOPOLDO
> I just came to warn you.

SAMANTHA shakes her head.

> SAMANTHA
> So, I'm not dreaming...

> LEOPOLDO
> You are...

LEOPOLDO hugs SAMANTHA.

> LEOPOLDO (CONT'D)
> They need you. Go and help
> them.

LEOPOLDO kisses SAMANTHA's head.

INT. BEDROOM - NIGHT

SAMANTHA is sleeping.

> LEOPOLDO (OS)
> *Sam... Sam... Wake up.*
> *Sam... Wake up.*

SAMANTHA opens her eyes, turns her head towards the couch. It is empty. SAMANTHA gets out of the bed and leaves the bedroom.

INT. LIVING ROOM - NIGHT

SAMANTHA enters the living room.

MAN 1 and MAN 2 are pointing their GUNS at DAMASCO and NADOC who are in front of them. NORA is behind the settee.

MAN 1 and MAN 2 look at SAMANTHA.

> MAN 2
> *(not moving his lips)*
> It's her!

> MAN 1
> *(not moving his lips)*
> Yeah, it's her, Kill'er.

MAN 1 and MAN 2 aim at SAMANTHA with their GUNS.

> SAMANTHA
> *(whispering)*
> Without Blood...

SAMANTHA puts her hands on her forehead. The GUNS fall down. NADOC makes two energy balls, each on one hand, SAMANTHA closes her eyes. MAN 1 and MAN 2 vanish and BUBBLES appear in their place. NADOC'S energy balls disappear.

NORA stands up and looks at SAMANTHA. DAMASCO and NADOC look at SAMANTHA. SAMANTHA leaves the living room.

Everything goes black.

END OF ACT 3

About Zathori's Spell

CHARACTERS

MAIN CHARACTERS

SAMANTHA (30), journalist. She works at
BOOKING BOOKS, a literary agency and a
magazine. She enjoys a normal life. She's
pregnant and happily married with Damasco. Her
life stops being ordinary when she hears two
people talking by mental telepathy. From that
moment she will try to have a normal life
while she will have to deal with her magic
life, like she had to do when she was a
teenager.

DAMASCO (34), webmaster and computer
technician. He works at home. He is taller
than SAMANTHA and athletic. He is a quiet
person who can focus on a task even when there
is a lot of trouble and noise. When he was a
teenager, he gave up his powers to be with
Samantha. He is happily married to Samantha
and they are expecting a baby. He will try to
protect his family from some people with bad
intentions. At first, he feels helpless
because he has sort of forgotten his powers.
He will have to learn how to summon them and
how to use them.

NADOC (32). He is a cheerful person. He is
from ZATHORI. He used to be a warrior when he
was young. When peace finally came, he became
a personal trainer: he helps people to get
fit, advises on nutritional habits and also
how to manage their powers and how to get them

back. He comes back into Samantha's and
Damasco's life. He will try to protect them
and help Damasco to win his powers back.

NORA (30). She is the best friend of Samantha
and a colleague at the magazine. She loves
romance books. She is very cheerful. She knows
about Samantha's magic past life.

BLANCA (60). She is Samantha's mother. She is
a writer and has the power of mental telepathy
though Samantha doesn't know it yet or has
forgotten. She loves crochet.

OTHER CHARACTERS:

LEOPOLDO (85). He is Blanca's father and
Samantha's grandfather. He lives in Zathori.
He disappeared when Samantha was a little
girl. They met again when she was 15. Leopoldo
was kidnapped and Samantha rescued him.

NERIUS (55). He is from Zathori and lives
there. He has dark hair and dark eyes. He
likes to dress in black and enjoy a healthy
life.

PACO (48). Manager at Nostrum cafeteria. He is
married with Tayri. He is from Venezuela. He
is a very cheerful person.

TAYRI (46). She works at Nostrum cafeteria.
She is married with Paco. She is from
Venezuela. She likes her customers to have a
good time in the cafeteria.

ANDREW (28). He is an attractive man who works at Nostrum cafeteria.

BOSS (50). He is benevolent and thinks his employees work well if there is flexibility.

DOCTOR (60). Episodic character.

PLACES

HOME: A flat in Chamberí, an area from Madrid, Spain. It is not a small flat nor a big flat either. BLANCA wants SAMANTHA and DAMASCO to move to another flat with her but SAMANTHA disagrees.

PARK: It is situated in another area of Madrid. SAMANTHA traveled from there to ZATHORI when she was a teenager. She used to go there when she was little girl, but she stopped when peace came to Zathori.

BOOKING BOOKS: It is the magazine and a literary agency where SAMANTHA and NORA work at. Their magazine is about books, new releases, reviews, authors, interviews,...

NOSTRUM: It is a cafeteria and a wholefood restaurant. It is close to the magazine. The characters go there a lot.

EPISODES

EPISODE 1. Magic's Back

Act 1 - SAMANTHA falls asleep at the office
and she has a flashback: She is 8 years old
and she is at the Retiro PARK with BLANCA
(38), her mother. She has thrown a BALL into
the pond. She wakes up and she goes with NORA
to Nostrum CAFETERIA to take a break. There
they meet ANDREW, the new employee, an
attractive man who Nora can't take her eyes
off. Then they go back to work.

SAMANTHA is at her desk and she hears
LEOPOLDO's voice calling her. Everything goes
black.

Act 2 - SAMANTHA is at the hospital with NORA
and DAMASCO. The DOCTOR (60) tells her that
she needs to rest. He also tells them that she
has a baby girl.

SAMANTHA goes home and takes a nap. She has
another FLASHBACK. In fact, it's the sequel of
the previous one she had when she fell asleep
at the office: Samantha's ball is in the pond
and we hear her saying: "Mum, it's just a
ball". NADOC (10) appears and tells them he
can recover the ball with his butterfly net.

SAMANTHA goes to work. She talks to her BOSS
(50) and they agree she will rest at home and
read a book during that week.

SAMANTHA is sat in the train returning home.
She hears two people talking about killing a
person. She looks at them and she sees that
they are still speaking but they are not
moving their mouths.

Act 3 - SAMANTHA is crying with DAMASCO next
to her trying to comfort her. Someone rings
the main door bell. It's NADOC (32).

Someone rings the door. NORA pays a visit to
SAMANTHA and meets NADOC. SAMANTHA doesn't
like the idea of having magic back in her
life. DAMASCO understands it and NADOC tells
her that it is something she cannot avoid.
SAMANTHA is not sure now of what she heard and
saw. DAMASCO reminds her that she needs to
rest.

SAMANTHA and NORA are in the bedroom. SAMANTHA
is on the bed reading "Without Blood" by
Alessandro Baricco while NORA is sat down on
the couch reading "The Yellow Bag" by Lygia
Bojunga Nunes.

SAMANTHA is sleeping. She dreams about
LEOPOLDO who tells her Damasco, Nadoc and Nora
need their help. We hear the voice of LEOPOLDO
calling her and telling her to wake up.
SAMANTHA opens her eyes and turns her head to
see NORA but she's not there. SAMANTHA goes to
the living room and she watches the two MEN
she saw on the train each with GUNS, DAMASCO
and NADOC in front of them and NORA behind a
settee. The two MEN look at SAMANTHA and they
say with mental telepathy that she's the one
they have to kill. SAMANTHA whispers: "Without
Blood", puts her hands on her forehead and the
GUNS of the two MEN fall to the floor. They
all look surprised at her. NADOC makes two
energy balls with his hands , each in one
hand. SAMANTHA closes her eyes. MAN 1 and MAN
2 vanish and BUBBLES appear in their places.
NADOC'S energy balls disappear.

SAMANTHA leaves the room.

Everything goes black.

EPISODE 2. Don't Blink

Act 1 - SAMANTHA and DAMASCO are having
breakfast in the living room. The doorbell
RINGS. It's BLANCA (60). BLANCA joins them for
breakfast and tells them about her latest trip
and her latest romance.

The doorbell RINGS again. It's NADOC. He
greetes BLANCA who smiles and embraces him.

SAMANTHA tells BLANCA that she's pregnant and
it's a girl. BLANCA kisses SAMANTHA and
DAMASCO. Then she sits down, opens her bag and
takes out a crochet needle and a white chunky
crochet yarn. BLANCA starts to crochet. BLANCA
asks SAMANTHA if she likes white for the baby
cot. SAMANTHA nods.

DAMASCO looks at NADOC and they both leave the
living room to give SAMANTHA and BLANCA some
time to themselves.

DAMASCO and NADOC are in Damasco's studio.
DAMASCO is typing code on his computer while
NADOC is reading a book.

NORA is inside Nostrum Cafeteria at a table
writing a WhatsApp to Samantha: "I hope you
and my niece are doing fine. I'm okay".

ANDREW serves a cup of coffee to NORA with a
smile on his face. NORA looks at him and
smiles back. NORA's smartphone BUZZES. NORA
opens the WhatsApp. It's SAMANTHA: "We are
fine but come asap. Something's going on".

NORA looks back at ANDREW, who is still
smiling.

ANDREW accompanies NORA outside the cafeteria.
He leans down and kisses NORA on the cheek.

NORA enters her PINK car, starts the engine,
waves goodbye to ANDREW and leaves.

BLANCA has made a crochet basket and gives it
to SAMANTHA who looks at it, smiles and
embraces BLANCA.

The doorbell RINGS. SAMANTHA opens the door.
It's NORA. SAMANTHA and NORA go to the living
room. NORA and BLANCA embrace.

DAMASCO asks NADOC to help him win his powers
back. NADOC agrees.

BLANCA leaves the living room, goes to her
room, takes a present for SAMANTHA and asks
DAMASCO and NADOC to follow her. They all go
to the living room and sit down. BLANCA gives
the present to SAMANTHA, who unwraps it. It's
a book: It's the Book of Shadows.

Act 2 - BLANCA teaches SAMANTHA how to use the
Book of Shadows. NORA supports BLANCA.

NORA goes back to work.

NADOC coaches DAMASCO to recover his powers.

ANDREW talks to a WARLOCK and tell him he will
send 4 WINKERS to the house.

SAMANTHA doesn't like the idea of having magic
back in her life. BLANCA asks her, without
moving her lips: "Why not?" SAMANTHA looks at
BLANCA who tells her she must learn how to use
magic just in case more demons decide to
attack her.

BLANCA coaches SAMANTHA and they find a spell
which will make a winker disappear.

Act 3 - The 4 WINKERS appear inside the house,
in the living room, and have fireballs in
their hands. BLANCA holds SAMANTHA's hand and
they both chant a spell. Two of the WINKERS
vanish leaving a trace of BUBBLES.

NADOC and DAMASCO already have fireballs in
their hands and throw them at the remaining
WINKERS, who disappear leaving a trace of
smoke.

When it's over, they all hug and NADOC asks
about the bubbles.

ANDREW talks to the WARLOCK who is angry with
him. ANDREW kills the WARLOCK with an ATHAME
and gets the Warlock's energy. ANDREW hires a
CHANGING SHAPE which uses NORA's form to get
closer to SAMANTHA.

EPISODE 3. I'm In Shape

SAMANTHA studies the Book of Shadows and
practises potions. BLANCA is helping her.

DAMASCO and NADOC are working at home trying
to create a security system: a human and a
magic one.

ANDREW has a date with NORA while the CHANGING
SHAPE goes to Samantha's home.

EPISODE 4. Power of a Woman

A VENEFICA is interested in SAMANTHA's powers whatever they are.

BLANCA releases SAMANTHA's powers. SAMANTHA discovers that the power of mind-hearing comes from the baby and it will evolve to full mental telepathy. But she's got another power and she doesn't know which it is.

EPISODE 12.

SAMANTHA gives birth to a lovely girl. When they come back home from the hospital, they see ANDREW in the living room. Despite the fact that NORA wants to believe that her lover is there for good reasons, she knows in her heart that he has used her. She tells them who he is and a battle starts. Finally, DAMASCO and NADOC win the fight. SAMANTHA, then agrees to move to another house where they will be safer.

From episode 1 to episode 12 of the first season, there are several things **THE CHARACTERS MUST LEARN:**

- SAMANTHA: Living an ordinary life is not for everybody and everything happens for a reason.

- DAMASCO: Fear can be a positive energy if you use it correctly.

- NADOC: Love can be anywhere.

- NORA: Some people are good, while some
people are evil.

- BLANCA: Children grow up.

WITCHES

There are good witches and bad witches.

BENANDANTI (Good Walkers)
They are white witches from Italy who fight evil witches (malandanti).

BRAG (Female Shape-Changer)
A woman who can disguise herself by changing into another form.

CHANGING SHAPE
A person who can take the form of animals. If they get injured in that form, they retain evidence of the injury when they return to human shape.

LAMIA
It has the head and torso of a woman but the other half of her body is serpent-like.

LILITH
She is a female demon very jealous of other women.

FASCINATRIX (Bewitchers)
Witches who could bewitch a man just with a glance.

MALEFICA
A witch who inflicts pain and terror on her victims.

SEA WITCH (Ghost of a Dead Witch)
She inhabits coastal waters and likes to lure
sailors into traps and to let them die.

STREGA
A female vampire who takes action at nights.
Their spells are cast on men.

WARLOCK
A male witch.

TOOLS

ATHAME
Knife which has a double-edged blade, a black
hilt and magic symbols on it.

GRIMOIRES
Books of magic spells and incantations owned
by wizards and sorcerers. An old grimoire is:
Key of Solomon[1].

PENTACLES AND PENTAGRAMS
They are used to conjure up spirits and as
protection.

Pentacle meaning:

Oxford Dictionaries: "A talisman or magical
object, typically disc-shaped and inscribed
with a pentagram, used as a symbol of the
element of earth."[2]

Collins Dictionary: "Another name for
pentagram."[3]

Pentagram meaning:

Oxford Dictionaries: "A five-pointed star that
is formed by drawing a continuous line in five

---

[1] https://en.wikipedia.org/wiki/Key_of_Solomon
[2] https://en.oxforddictionaries.com/definition/pentacle
[3] https://www.collinsdictionary.com/dictionary/english/pentacle

straight segments, often used as a mystic and
magical symbol."[4]

Collins Dictionary: "A star-shaped figure
formed by extending the sides of a regular
pentagon to meet at five points. Such a figure
used as a magical or symbolic figure by the
Pythagoreans, black magicians, etc. Also
called: pentacle, pentangle."[5]

Cambridge Dictionary: "A star with five
points, drawn using five straight lines,
sometimes used as a symbol of magic."[6]

Dictionary.com: "A five-pointed, star-shaped
figure made by extending the sides of a
regular pentagon until they meet, used as an
occult symbol by the Pythagoreans and later
philosophers, by magicians, etc."[7]

PINS
Bent pins were used in potions to cast or to
break spells.

---

[4] https://en.oxforddictionaries.com/definition/pentagram
[5] https://www.collinsdictionary.com/dictionary/english/pentagram
[6] http://dictionary.cambridge.org/es/diccionario/ingles/pentagram
[7] http://www.dictionary.com/browse/pentagram?s=t

FAMILIARS

A familiar is a spirit which helps the witch in their magic duties.

The usual familiars were cats and dogs but they could be other animals.

The familiar could be inherited or acquired when another witch gave it up to the witch voluntarily.

SPELLS

BOOK OF SHADOWS
It's the witch's bible of witchcraft where she could find chants, spells, incantations, rituals,… and also add new information to it.

CURSES
Magic spells to bring misfortune to other people.

ESBATS
Regular meetings of witches. They were held at night when the moon was full. They took place outdoors a witch's house. Food and drink was shared.

EVIL EYE
It's a spell casted involuntarily or deliberately.

FASCINATION
The victim surrenders to the witch's will by a process similar to hypnosis.

GREAT RITE
It symbolizes the union between a man and a woman, within a magic circle at a Sabbat or other meeting. The High Priest puts his ritual knife into a cup.

HANDFASTING
It's the witch's wedding and the couple is bound together as long as they love each other. They exchange gold or silver rings.

HANDPARTING
It's the witch's equivalent of divorce.

HEDGE WITCHES
Solitary witches who used the power of natural
remedies for the benefit of their community.

LIGHT AND DARKNESS
The forces of LIGHT were at their most
powerful on the longest day of the year, and
the forces of DARKNESS on the shortest day of
the year.

MAGIC WORDS
Witches used magical incantations to summon up
a spirit.

NECROMANCY
The spirits of the dead roam freely. Witches
can use them to find missing items or to find
out the cause of their death.

SABBATS
The Spring Equinox (March 21)
Beltane (April 20)
The Summer Solstice (June 21)
Lamas (July 31)
The Autumn Equinox (September 21)
Samhain (October 31)
The Summer Solstice (December 21)

SPELLS
Witches use them to create or change a course
of events. If a word rhymed it increased the
power of the spell.
Positive spells, such as blessings or
enchantments, are cast for protection,
healing, love,…

Spells for negative use cause misfortune and
illness.…

WELLS
Entrance to the realms of the fairies.

PLANTS

Witches use plants for their potions and spells. They can use them for protection, to poison or kill the enemy, to increase the power of their magical tools, to provide physical strength

APPLES (Genus Malus)

BELLADONNA (Atropa belladonna)

ELDER (Sambucus nigra)

FERN (Genus Aspleniaceae)

ERGOT (Claviceps purpurea)

FOXGLOVE (Digitalis purpurea)

FENNEL (Foeniculum vulgare)

HAWTHORN (Crataegus oxyacantha)

HEATHER (Calluna vulgaris)

HELLEBORE (Helleborus niger)

HEMP (Cannabis sativa)

HENBANE (Hyoscyamus niger)

JIMSON WWED (Datura stramonium)

LETTUCE (Genus Lactuca)

MANDRAKE (Atropa mandragora)

MISTLETOE (Viscum album)

MONKSHOOD (Aconitum napellus)

ORANGE (Citrus vulgaris)

POPPY (Papaver rhoeas)

PURPLE ORCHIS (Habenaria fimbriata)

ROWAN (Pyrus aucuparia)

RUE (Ruta graveolens)

SCARLET PIMPERNEL (Anagallis arvensis)

SPEEDWELL (Veronica officinalis)

TOBACCO (Nicotianam tabacum)

TRAILING PEARLWORT (Sagina decumbens)

VERVAIN (Verbena officinalis)

WATER LILY (Genus Nymphaca)

WOODBINE (Gelsemium nitidum)

YARROW (Achillea millefolium)

SOURCES

Pentacle. (n.d.). Online Etymology Dictionary.
Retrieved August 14, 2017 from Dictionary.com
website
http://www.dictionary.com/browse/pentacle

Canwell, Diane; Sutherland Jonathan; *Witches
of the World*, 2008

https://en.wikipedia.org/wiki/Key_of_Solomon

https://en.oxforddictionaries.com/definition/p
entacle

https://www.collinsdictionary.com/dictionary/e
nglish/pentacle

https://en.oxforddictionaries.com/definition/p
entagram

https://www.collinsdictionary.com/dictionary/e
nglish/pentagram

http://dictionary.cambridge.org/es/diccionario
/ingles/pentagram

http://www.dictionary.com/browse/pentagram?s=t

ABOUT JADINE TYNE

Thank you very much for reading **Zathori's Spell**. This is my first book published in English and I'm planning to publish more in this language.

My previous book was written in Spanish: **A pocos centímetros**. If you can read in this language, I recommend you to read it.

https://www.amazon.es/dp/B06XKCLMXW

I invite you to visit my website, follow me on the social network and subscribe to my newsletter where you'll access to additional contents and giveaways.

www.JadineTyne.com

ABOUT ME

- **I am:** JADINE TYNE, screenwriter of short films and TV series.
- **I love:** writing fiction.
- **I'll always be:** a writer.
- **I don't like:** not having time for reading and writing.
- **I won't be:** a person who brag or who sells illusion.

- **I want to be**: a full time writer, a job
  which will keep me independent instead of
  writing as a hobby. I don't mind dealing
  with marketing and design as part of my
  job.

ACKNOLEDGMENTS

I want to thank the support received from my
family: my husband Antonio and my son Leo.
They are just there, next to me. They know
that projects take time to be finished.

Thanks to my Bertrand family and Envíos
Tricolor. They always support me and help me
out when it's necessary.

Thank you to the cast and crew of the
Zathori's Spell opening scene shooting: María
José Marín García (majoworks7), Patricia
Bertrand, José María Velasco, Iván Roche, Katy
Bertrand and, last but not least, Ada
Rodríguez del Castillo.

Finally, I want to thank Tim, Steve, Roger
(Roger Orr) and Patrick. They taught me not
only English language but their culture too. I
still remember when we played cricket in
class!!

www.JadineTyne.com

www.JadineTyne.com

www.JadineTyne.com

www.ingramcontent.com/pod-product-compliance
Lightning Source LLC
LaVergne TN
LVHW010653200726
843507LV00011B/1854

9 788846 977085